LAN

TO THE RESCUE!

 **Greenwillow Books**
An Imprint of HarperCollins*Publishers*

Plum to the Rescue!
Text and illustrations copyright © 2024 by Matt Phelan

The text of this book is set in Charlotte Book.
Book design by Sylvie Le Floc'h

Library of Congress Cataloging-in-Publication Data

Names: Phelan, Matt, author.
Title: Plum to the rescue! / written and illustrated by Matt Phelan.
Description: First edition. I New York : Greenwillow Books, an Imprint of HarperCollins Publishers, 2024. I Audience: Ages 8-12. I Audience: Grades 2-3. I Summary: When one of Plum's peachick wards fall into the hands of the notorious Bickle brats, he and his friends at the Athensville Zoo set out to rescue her.
Identifiers: LCCN 2024004848 (print) I LCCN 2024004849 (ebook) I ISBN 9780063296299 (hardcover) I ISBN 9780063296312 (ebook)
Subjects: CYAC: Zoos—Fiction. I Peacocks—Fiction. I Animals—Infancy—Fiction. I Animals—Fiction. I Kidnapping—Fiction. I LCGFT: Animal fiction.
Classification: LCC PZ7.P44882 Pl 2024 (print) I LCC PZ7.P44882 (ebook) I DDC [Fic]—dc23
LC record available at https://lccn.loc.gov/2024004848
LC ebook record available at https://lccn.loc.gov/2024004849
24 25 26 27 28 LBC 5 4 3 2 1
First Edition

 Greenwillow Books

For Nora

**Chapter One
The Pitter-Patter
of Tiny Talons**

Ah, springtime. Is there any finer season? And spring is at its very finest at the Athensville Zoo. On this particular Saturday, the air was sweet, the flower beds were in bloom, and everyone had two words on their minds:

Zoo babies!

Yes, the zoo was full of new young animals.

Three lion cubs, a baby gorilla, a giraffe calf, two snow leopard cubs, a wee little aardvark, and . . .

"Peachicks!"

Hampstead, head peacock at the Athensville Zoo, stood addressing *most* of the flock at the (ahem) Mandatory Morning Meeting.

"Where are the peachicks?" Hampstead said. "Who is looking after them?"

A jaunty chirp rang through the air. Plum the

peppy purple peacock marched around the Great Tree followed by five skipping peachicks.

"Toodle pip, my friends!" Plum called to the gathered flock.

"Peep! Peep! Peep! Peep!" said four of the peachicks.

"Pip!" said the fifth and smallest chick.

"Very good," Plum said to the little chick.

"Plum!" said Hampstead. "The chicks must learn that attendance at the morning meeting is *mandatory*."

"Of course," said Plum. "We just took the long way around."

"Why did you do that?" demanded Hampstead.

"Because it's more fun!" said Plum. "I'm Fun Plum! That rhymes . . . sort of."

"Peep! Peep! Peep! Peep! Pip!" said the peachicks.

"You certainly are fun," said Judy, the chicks' mother. "They adore you."

"Especially the little one," added Bill, the father. "All she says now is 'pip.' In fact, we decided to name her Pip."

"Perfect!" said Plum.

"Listen, Fun Plum," said Judy. "Bill and I could use a rest. Would you mind taking the chicks out for a stroll around the zoo?"

"You betcha!" said Plum. "I'll show them the ropes, give them the skinny, the lowdown, the lay of the land."

"Thanks," said the two tired parents. They hopped up into the Great Tree for a much-needed nap.

"Righty-o, peachicks," said Plum. "Are you ready for excitement and thrills?"

"About that," said Hampstead.

"Uh-oh," said Plum.

"No thrills, Plum," said Hampstead. "A quiet bit of exercise and, most importantly, careful and complete supervision at all times."

"*Super*vision . . ." said Plum. "Oooh, I wish I had super vision. I could see the moon up close! Or all the latest toys inside the souvenir shop!"

"Focus, Plum," said Hampstead. "This calls for serious attention. These chicks are your responsibility today."

"Uh-huh," said Plum.

"You are *responsible* for their safety," said Hampstead slowly.

"Sure am!" said Plum.

"Plum," said Hampstead.

"Yes, Hampstead?" said Plum.

"The chicks are wandering away."

Plum turned. All five chicks had indeed toddled and skipped down the path.

"Oh, so they have. The little firecrackers!"

"Meg!" called Hampstead.

Meg strolled over.

"Hi, Hampstead. Hi, Plum!"

"Hiya, Meg!"

"Meg, would you please help Plum watch the chicks?" Hampstead asked.

"Sure," said Meg.

"Okay," said Plum. "But remember, Hampstead, the chicks are *my* responsibility. *I* am the responsible one."

"Harrumph," said Hampstead.

"*Responsibility* is my middle name," continued Plum.

Hampstead sighed and hopped up into the Great Tree.

"Fun 'Responsibility' Plum, that's me!" Plum called after him.

Meg laughed. "I think he gets the idea, Plum."

"I could go on."

"I'm sure you could," said Meg. "But the chicks just turned the corner."

"Oh," said Plum. "We should probably catch up."

"I think that's best," said Meg.

Chapter Two
Super Vision
in Action

Plum and Meg caught up with the chicks and made them stand in an orderly line.

"Okay, little chicks, a word of caution from your totally responsible—but still fun—supervisor," said Plum.

"Pip!" said Pip.

"No, Pip, it will not take long, I promise," said Plum.

"Pip!"

"Peachicks," said Plum solemnly. "You are now part of the amazing, stupendous, fabulously wonderful Athensville Zoo."

The chicks peeped excitedly.

"Within these hallowed walls," said Plum, swirling around with outstretched wings, "you are completely safe!"

"Mention the lions," said Meg.

"I will," said Plum, hopping onto a statue of a large tortoise.

"And the tigers," added Meg.

"Yes, as Meg points out," continued Plum, "some of our animals can be a tad bitey. You will learn to keep a safe and respectful distance."

"Peeeeep," said the chicks in a worried tone.

"They are all friends," said Plum quickly.

"Unless they're hungry," muttered Meg.

"Unless they're hungry," said Plum.

The chicks quivered and huddled together.

"Never fear, little ones," said Plum. "You have a fine peacock flock and wonderful keepers to look after you!"

Lizzie, Plum and Meg's favorite keeper, walked down the path at that moment.

"Aw!" said Lizzie, joining them. "The peachicks!"

"Peep! Peep! Peep! Peep! Pip!"

"How adorable," said Lizzie. "You two taking good care of them?"

"I'm mostly in charge, Lizzie," chirped Plum. "Meg is helping."

"Right," said Meg. "Helping."

Lizzie couldn't actually understand them, but she knew Meg and Plum enough to trust them.

"You are in good hands—er, wings—with Plum and Meg," she said to the chicks. "Follow them and you can't go wrong."

She turned to Meg and Plum.

"You two are lucky to have each other. I hope Jeremy doesn't get lonely in the apartment when I'm here at work." Lizzie sighed. "Well . . . I better get back to my rounds."

Jeremy was a former street cat and now Lizzie's

happy indoor cat. He was also one of Plum and Meg's best friends.

"Oh, poor Jeremy," said Meg. "I hope he isn't lonely."

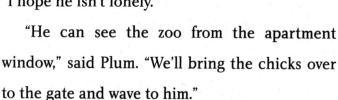

"He can see the zoo from the apartment window," said Plum. "We'll bring the chicks over to the gate and wave to him."

Meg looked around. The chicks were gone.

"We'll need to find them first."

"See, Meg," said Plum. "They already feel safe in the zoo."

"Uh-huh," said Meg. "Let's hurry, Plum."

They didn't need to look for long. All five peachicks were farther down the path. A bit of pink cotton candy had fallen to the ground, and the chicks were pushing it around like a ball.

After successfully separating the chicks from the sticky cotton candy, Plum and Meg continued the tour.

They visited the new baby gorilla, who was snuggling with her mama.

They quietly admired the baby aardvark, who was taking a nap.

And they paid their respects to the lion cubs, who were certainly more cute than scary.

The next stop was the Small and Unusual Mammal Pavilion, so the chicks could meet the zoo's one and only ningbing, Itch.

"Hmm," said Itch, inspecting the chicks. "A bit small, but I suppose they are healthy enough."

"Pip!" said Pip.

"We think they are a wonderful addition to the family," said a proud Plum.

"*Flock,* not *family,*" corrected Itch. "And I am not convinced that we needed additional peacocks."

"Luckily that is not your call," said Meg.

"Do you ever imagine what it would be like if I *did* make the decisions at the zoo?" said Itch. A dreamy look crossed his little face. "If all animals and keepers hung on my every word, ready to follow my lead without question?"

"Can't say I have ever imagined that, Itch," said Meg.

"I'm trying right now," said Plum. "But it's a bit murky."

Itch sighed. "Off you go now. Leave me alone to dream of greatness."

"You got it, Itch," said Plum. "Peacocks! Move on out!"

The peacocks crossed the zoo, pausing for photos with various guests and ending up by the Prairie Dog Pound.

"Well, that's about it," said Plum. "This is your world, the Athensville Zoo!"

"There *is* a whole world beyond the zoo walls, little chicks," said Meg.

"Yes . . . ," said Plum. "But it's best to stay here where it's safe."

"Not everywhere is dangerous, Plum," said Meg. She turned back to the peachicks.

"We have lots of animal friends in the woods. Every full moon, we all gather here for the Shindig. You'll meet chipmunks, raccoons, a bear named ThunderPaws. . . ."

"Oooh," said the chicks.

"But the zoo animals—like you—stay within these walls. This is where we belong," said Plum.

"That is true," said Meg. "This is our home.

The chicks peeped and pipped happily.

"It's about time for lunch. We should get back to the Great Tree," said Meg.

"Awwww!" said the chicks.

"Awwww!" said Plum. "Just a little longer, pleeeease?"

"All right, Fun Plum," said Meg. "Are you okay getting them back on your own?"

"Without a doubt," said Plum. "Right, chicks?"

"See you soon," said Meg. She waved and walked in the direction of the Great Tree.

"Pip! Pip!"

Pip, the littlest peachick, wandered over

to inspect the Prairie Dog Pound. The others followed.

"This is where the prairie dogs live," said Plum. "I don't see any of them right now. Those mounds lead down to tunnels that run through the whole zoo!"

"Pip?"

"Sure, I guess you can check them out," said Plum.

Pip wiggled down a mound opening. The rest of the chicks popped down other mounds.

Plum peeked down.

"Cool, huh?" said Plum. "I wish I was still small enough to fit in those tunnels."

The chicks scampered through the tunnels. Plum sat down to wait. Then he stood. Then he hopped a bit. Then he flapped his wings real fast. He popped his plumage out and back in.

Waiting was getting boring.

"Hiya, Plum!" Kevin the giant elephant shrew called down from his elevated habitrail.

"Ahoy, Kevin!" said Plum. "I'm watching the peachicks."

"I don't see any peachicks, Plum," said Kevin.

"They're exploring the tunnels."

"Oh," said Kevin. "That's super fun."

"I know!"

"Guess what?" said Kevin. "The baby giraffe is taking her first steps."

"Wow!" said Plum.

"Come watch!" said Kevin, racing down his habitrail.

"Can't miss that!" said Plum, and he ran toward the giraffe pen.

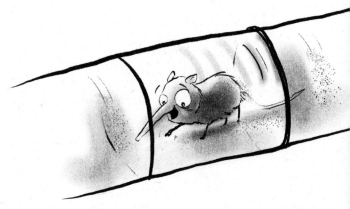

Chapter Three
The Bickle Brats

Across the grounds, a family with two children entered the gates. These children sent a shiver down the spines of all who worked or lived at the Athensville Zoo.

"The Bickle brats!" exclaimed a peacock named Terry.

Why did Terry refer to these children by the

not-so-nice name of *brat*? Because, if there were ever children who lived up to that description, Rodney Bickle and his little sister, Betty Bickle, were those children.

If a pen had an observation window, Rodney and Betty banged on it.

If an animal was small and timid, Rodney and Betty yelled at it.

If there was a line at the carousel, Rodney and Betty cut it.

If an unfortunate peacock crossed their path,

Rodney and Betty chased it. And chased it. And chased it.

Then there were the tantrums.

The Bickle family had been politely asked to leave the zoo

several times. But they always returned, and everyone—keepers, animals, peacocks, guests—quaked with fear at the bad behavior that was sure to come with them.

At the giraffe pen, a happy crowd cheered the baby giraffe as she wobbled by her mother's side. They were all blissfully unaware of the arrival of the Bickle brats.

"You can do it, Sally!" called Plum. "Woo-hoo!"

"Look at her go!" said Kevin from his habitrail above. "Yay, Sally!"

Terry skittered up to Plum.

"Plum," squeaked Terry. "The Bickle brats have entered the zoo!"

"Yikes," said Plum, leaping into the air. "I thought they were banned until summer."

"Guess not," said Terry.

"Where are they now?" asked Plum.

"They didn't get far. Both kids demanded to be taken into the first souvenir shop, the one right by the gates."

"That should buy us some time," said Plum. "Hey, Kevin! Spread the word!"

"I'm on it!" said Kevin. "Gee, I'm glad my habitrail is several feet off the ground."

"Lucky you," said Terry. "I'll gather the peacocks and we can meet back at the Great Tree. Bring the chicks, Plum!"

The chicks.

"Uh-oh," said Plum.

Chapter Four
A Tunnel of Fun

Plum hurried back to the Prairie Dog Pound. The peachicks were safe, of course. The Bickle brats couldn't get into the tunnels.

But he'd better check on them. Just in case.

"PLUM!"

Hampstead beckoned from beneath the statue of Plato, the first peacock of the Athensville Zoo.

"Those ruffians are back in our midst," said Hampstead. "And—no surprise—I see you are *not* with our chicks!"

"All is well, Hampstead," said Plum, jogging in place to keep up his momentum. "Getting them now!"

"You *do* know where they are?"

"Yes. Well . . . in a manner of speaking. Gotta run!"

Plum left Hampstead sputtering.

"Oh, Plum!"

What now?

Bill and Judy, the peachicks' parents, peeked out from behind a bench.

"Ah!" said Plum. "Just gathering the chicks now! I'll see you back at the Great Tree."

"Thanks, Plum," said Bill. "We knew we could count on you."

"Uh-huh," said Plum. He sped around the bend. The Prairie Dog Pound was in sight.

"Plum!"

Plum skidded to a stop in front of Meg.

"Where are the chicks? It's a code red Bickle emergency!" said Meg.

"I know!" said Plum. "They're in the prairie dog tunnels."

"The tunnels!" exclaimed Meg. "Those run all under the zoo!"

"Don't remind me," said Plum.

Plum and Meg raced to the Prairie Dog Pound. Plum leaned over one of the mounds.

"All peachicks! Time to go!"

They waited.

Plum glanced at Meg.

Meg glanced at Plum.

And then . . .

"Peep! Peep! Peep! Peep!"

Little peachicks scrambled happily out of the mounds.

"See, Meg?" said Plum. "Nothing to worry about."

"Plum," said Meg. "There are four chicks here."

"Yep," said Plum.

"We have *five* chicks."

"Oh."

Plum turned back to the mound.

"Which one is missing?"

"Pip. The littlest one," said Meg. "The one that looks up to you the most."

"Right." Plum took a deep breath and yelled into the mound, "Piiiiiiiiip!"

A furry little head poked out of the tunnel.

"Jeez Louise, Plum! You busted my eardrums," said the prairie dog.

"Sorry, Dave," said Plum. "I'm looking for Pip,

a peachick. Have you seen her?"

"Oh, sure. She's the brave one. She plowed through the tunnels without a lick of fear."

"Where is she now?"

"She went all the way to the end of the south tunnel, then took the exit up to the surface.

"What?" yelled Meg.

"Where does the south tunnel end?" asked Plum.

"The souvenir shop," said Dave. "The one by the front gate."

The Bickle brats had set a new record. Moments after entering the zoo, they threw tantrums, demanding to be taken directly to the souvenir shop. Once inside the shop, they broke two monkey back scratchers, a plastic tiger that nodded its head, and a fairly expensive snow globe featuring a tiny replica of the zoo. Then they fought over a series of stuffed animals. When their parents refused to purchase two of each in the store, Rodney and Betty Bickle exploded in a five-alarm nuclear meltdown.

That was when Meg and Plum arrived on the scene, panting and out of breath.

"Good," said Plum over the noise that shook the walls of the souvenir shop. "They're still inside. Now let's find Pip and get out of here."

Rodney and Betty ran out of the shop in tears of rage. They began to circle the souvenir shop with increasing speed. Around and around they went, yelling and screaming.

And then the screaming stopped. Rodney and Betty were out of sight, behind the shop.

"Maybe one of the tigers is loose," said Meg.

After a moment the Bickle brats strolled serenely to the front of the shop where their parents stood.

"I guess they're trying to apologize," said Plum.

The parents were not convinced. The family headed toward the gates. Another record set.

"Whew," said Meg. "Now let's find—"

"Pip," said Plum in a hollow voice.

The Bickle brats were leaving the zoo early, without so much as an ice cream cone. Yet they were quiet and smiling.

And Plum knew why.

A tiny peachick peeked out of Rodney Bickle's drawstring backpack.

"Pip!" she squeaked.

Meg and Plum watched as the Bickle family

exited the gates with the kidnapped chick.

Plum raced forward, but a crowd of people were both coming and going through the gates. A ticket taker was stationed there.

"Plum, you'll never get past the crowd!" said Meg. "And you *can't* leave the zoo!"

"But—" said Plum.

"A keeper will notice. The Bickle parents will bring Pip back. We can't do anything right now."

"But," said Plum quietly, "she's my responsibility."

A voice sounded over the loudspeaker: "Good afternoon, Athensville Zoo! It is my great pleasure to inform you that our snow leopard mama is bringing her brand-new cubs out for a frolic! Come see the cuteness!"

The entire crowd made a beeline for the snow leopard pen. Even the ticket taker craned her neck, hoping to catch a glimpse.

Plum bolted through the gates.

"Plum, no!" cried Meg.

Plum ran faster than he ever had. He looked up at the gates on either side of him as he sped through the majestic zoo walls.

The wonderful, safe zoo walls.

"Focus, Plum," he said to himself.

He did not see the Bickle brats or Pip.

He didn't even see the street that he ran into.

Or the car fast approaching.

**Chapter Five
The Great Beyond**

SCREEECH!

The car slammed on the brakes and Plum jumped into the air. He landed, surrounded by other moving cars.

And then he was hit—not by a car, but by a soft, white cat.

"Plum! Get out of the street!" yelled his friend

Jeremy. "You have to be careful!"

Jeremy led Plum between the oncoming cars to the other side of the road.

"Jeremy!" said Plum. "How did you get here?"

"I saw the whole thing from Lizzie's window," said Jeremy. "So I opened the screen and came down the fire escape. It's super easy."

"Well, I am glad for that," said Plum. "I have to rescue Pip the peachick. The Bickle brats took her."

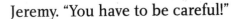

"Those kids are bad news," said Jeremy.

Plum scanned the parking lot. "They've driven away. Do you know where they live?"

"No," said Jeremy. "But other cats might. Everyone has heard of those two."

"What cats? Where?"

"My old home . . . the town dump," said Jeremy. "But, Plum, maybe this is a job for Lizzie or the Bickle parents."

"It's my job," said Plum firmly. "Take me to the dump. Please."

"Okay," said Jeremy. "Follow me."

Meanwhile, back in the zoo, Meg hadn't waited to see Plum cross the street. She had immediately run to find Lizzie, the zookeeper.

"What's up, Meg?" asked Lizzie.

FLAP! FLAP! FLAP!

"Are you hurt?"

FLAPPITY FLAPPITY FLAP!

"I'm sorry, I don't understand," said Lizzie.

"I'm more sorry," said Meg, and she darted away from the confused keeper.

Meg still believed that the Bickle parents would find and return Pip. But Plum outside the zoo on his own? He needed to be rescued. And she knew exactly the right animal for the job.

"Itch!" Meg mumbled, tapping Itch's window with the bent paper clip she held in her beak.

The Small and Unusual Mammal Pavilion had no visitors at the moment. Itch had taken the opportunity to practice his meditation.

"Meg," he said with eyes closed, "tapping is not helpful for my journey of inner peace."

"No time for peace," said Meg. "But you are going on a journey."

Meg quickly explained the situation.

"I'll exit the zoo via the secret chipmunk entrance in the northeast wall," said Itch. "I'll find Plum and bring him back."

"Please hurry," said Meg, and then she slipped the paper clip into the cage's lock.

Itch reached inside his little sleeping hut and pulled out a tight braid of leaves. It looked exactly like his tail. He placed it so some of the braid stuck out of the hut. "There. No one will notice my absence."

Meg managed to pick the lock and open the cage door. "We're getting really good at breaking rules," she said. "You're a bad influence on me, Itch."

"Birds of a feather, Meg. Birds of a feather,"

said the ningbing. "And now, let us make a hasty escape!"

Itch clung to Meg's back as she ran across the zoo to the northeast wall. At the base of the wall, there was a small crack. The crack was the entrance to a tiny passage to the outside world. Visiting chipmunks used it to attend the monthly Shindig.

"Good luck," said Meg. "We're counting on you."

"Plum saved me once," said Itch, remembering an eventful snowy day at Romeburg Elementary School. "Actually, Plum has saved me more than once . . . in different ways."

Itch scrambled through the passage and emerged on the other side of the wall. There were streets, cars, trees, houses, and stores, but no sign of Plum.

"It is likely that Plum will make his way to the Bickle residence," said Itch. "That's where I'll find him. But where do they live?"

Itch spotted a sewer opening at the corner of the sidewalk.

"Aha!" He scurried over and peered into the dark, smelly opening.

"If you want information, you go to the underworld!"

Itch dropped down to the sewers below.

Chapter Six
The Dump

Plum raced behind Jeremy as he led the way to the town dump. They stayed behind hedges and other natural cover as much as possible. But Plum wasn't worried about being spotted. Everything around him was a blur. Nothing mattered but rescuing Pip. How would he do it? Plum had no idea. But he would. He had to.

"Here we are," said Jeremy.

The Athensville Dump looked exactly how Plum had imagined it would. Piles of discarded stuff everywhere. Scrap metal. Broken glass. A few old cars.

"Stick close to me," said Jeremy. "There are some shady characters here."

Plum nodded and followed, stepping carefully over glass and debris.

"How long did you live here?" asked Plum.

"Too long." Jeremy sighed.

"Do you still have friends here?"

"I never had a friend until I met

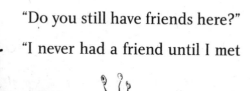

you," said Jeremy. "There were other cats, raccoons, rats, animals like that. But we all kept to ourselves."

"So who can help us?" asked Plum as he watched a snake slither under a heap of trash.

"I remember one cat, a real talker," said Jeremy. "He had a run-in with the Bickle brats."

"What's his name?"

"We don't have names out here, remember? You gave me the name Jeremy."

"Then how do we—"

"Hey!" called a voice. "I know you!"

A tan cat with stripes sat on top of an old refrigerator.

He blended in well with his surroundings. It took Plum a second to spot him.

"It's me! Bongo!" said the cat.

"Bongo?" said Jeremy.

"Yeah!" said the cat. "I gave myself a cool name. Bongo!"

"Oh. I have a name now, too. It's Jeremy."

"That's pretty good," said Bongo.

"Thanks," said Jeremy. "Listen, we were actually looking for you. We need some information and we're in a hurry."

"I'm not in a hurry," said Bongo. "I have loads of time. Want to know why?"

"Well," said Plum.

"It explains my cool name."

"But we really—" said Jeremy.

"This is the story of how I came to be called

Bongo the cat," said Bongo, leaping from the fridge onto an old washing machine.

"We're in a rush," said Plum.

"Story first," continued Bongo. "One day, *it* appeared in the dump." He paused and waited.

Plum sighed. "What appeared?"

"A bongo drum."

Pause.

"And so you decided to call yourself Bongo," said Jeremy, trying to speed up the story.

"No," said Bongo. "For three whole days I stared at that bongo drum. Three days. And then . . ."

"Then you played it," said Plum quickly.

"Nope. Then I *approached* it."

"And *then* you played it," said Jeremy.

"Uh-uh. I stared at it some more. But closer."

"And you decided to call yourself Bongo," said Plum.

"Not right away."

"You eventually played the bongo and had so much fun, and you loved the sound, and it added meaning to your life, and now you are called Bongo," declared Jeremy.

"I did not play it," said Bongo in a whisper.

Plum looked at Jeremy. They waited.

"I sat on it," said Bongo.

Another pause.

"Oooookay," said Plum.

"It was so smooth and cool to the touch. I sat on it for hours. But the story has a sad ending," said Bongo.

"But it does have an ending?" asked Plum.

"Some teenagers came to the dump one day,"

continued Bongo. "They found my bongo and took it away from me. And now . . ."

"Yes?" encouraged Jeremy.

"*I* am the Bongo of the dump."

They waited for more. Bongo scratched his ear.

"That's a really great story," said Plum cautiously. "I'm sorry about your bongo."

"Eh," said Bongo, leaping down from the washing machine. "Easy come, easy go in the dump. So, what can I do for you?"

"We need to know where the Bickle brats live," said Jeremy.

Bongo's eyes widened.

"Hoo boy! They're two scoops of trouble! I almost got caught there once. They wanted to feed me to their gigantic dog."

"They kidnapped one of our peachicks," said Plum.

"Are you a peacock? I thought you were some kind of colorful seagull. We get a lot of seagulls at the dump, which is weird since we're not near the sea."

"Can you take us there?"

"The sea?"

"No!" said Jeremy. "The Bickle house!"

"Oh, sure," said Bongo. "Like I said, I have plenty of time now that I don't have a cool bongo to sit on. Why didn't you say that in the first place?"

**Chapter Seven
The Yard**

Once again Plum found himself racing along at top speed, this time behind two cats. They went down alleys and side streets, behind garages, and through a park. They ran for a long time.

It occurred to Plum that he should have been paying attention to their route. He had no idea how to get back to the zoo. But the cats could lead them back. He wasn't worried about that.

He *was* worried about Pip. The poor little chick. She must be so scared. He picked up speed.

Bongo and Jeremy chatted as they ran.

"So, Jeremy," said Bongo. "A house cat now, huh?"

"An apartment cat. No more dumps for me, thank you."

"Does your home have any bongos?"

"No bongos."

"Oh, well," said Bongo. "Any other nice places to sit?"

"Sure! Chairs, a sofa, a bed, a nice ledge by the window, a kitchen counter, bathroom sink, top of fridge . . . lots of places."

"Imagine that," said Bongo.

They fell silent for a moment while waiting to cross a busy road.

"I always thought you were too cool to talk to," said Bongo.

"What? Me?" said Jeremy.

"You were the cool cat."

"No, *you* were the cool cat! You always had stories and adventures," said Jeremy.

"Huh," said Bongo.

"Huh," said Jeremy.

"Are we almost there?" panted Plum.

"Sure are, my peacock buddy," said Bongo. "The Bickle brats live at the end of this street. It's a dead end."

"Of course it is," said Jeremy.

"Come on!" said Plum.

"Whoa, whoa, whoa!" said Bongo. "You can't

just charge in there, especially with all of your colorful feathers."

"Bongo's right, Plum. We need to sneak up and check out the situation."

"But . . . ," said Plum.

"No buts, Plum," said Bongo. "This mission calls for a cat-style approach."

"Lots of caution, then quick action," explained Jeremy.

They crept up to the Bickle house. It was nice. A big house with a cheerful flower bed out front.

But the backyard was a different story.

The large, rectangular yard was surrounded by a high chain-link fence. Two sickly trees stood there, one outside the fence and the other inside the yard. Several piñatas hung from the branches of the second tree. They were shaped like a unicorn, a kitten, a rainbow, and a fairy princess. They were in pretty bad shape. Bats and sticks lay on the ground beneath the piñatas.

"Was there a birthday party?" asked Jeremy.

"No," said Bongo. "Those are always hanging there. The kids just like to whack them."

Plum shivered.

A run-down garden shed stood in the corner of the yard, surrounded by busted bicycles, deflated soccer balls and footballs, and other mangled sports equipment. Toys were scattered everywhere, but none of them looked remotely fun or functional. Rusty toy trucks with missing tires. Bent hula hoops. A narrow, wet, yellow strip of plastic ran down the center of the yard. A soft-tipped rocket was standing at a weird angle with a hose and a flat plastic ball tangled in front of it. There was also a small trampoline with a large hole in the middle.

"I don't see Pip or the kids," said Plum.

"They're probably inside," said Jeremy.

"Do you think they have Pip inside, too?" asked Plum.

"When the brats tried to catch me, they were going to keep me in that shed," said Bongo. "I got away before they could lock me in."

The shed door was shut. Was it locked? Could they force it open?

"I'm going to check the shed," said Plum.

"No," said Bongo.

"Why not?"

"Two reasons. One, I don't think you can get over this fence. And two, the yard is *not* deserted."

A low, rumbling growl came from under the back deck. A huge German shepherd emerged. It

was the largest, meanest-looking dog
Plum had ever seen.

"Meet Brick, family dog," said Bongo.

Brick barked. The sound was deafening
and fierce and terrifying.

Plum, Jeremy, and Bongo zipped behind a
nearby bush as Brick charged. He jumped up on
the fence, rattling it violently. But he couldn't get
over it. They were safe.

"Oh, my," said Plum.

The back door slammed open and Rodney and
Betty Bickle hopped down the stairs. Rodney was
holding his backpack.

"Quiet, Brick!" said Betty. The dog stopped barking.

The kids looked around. The coast was clear of
grown-ups. Rodney opened the drawstring pack
and pulled out little Pip.

"Pip?" she squeaked.

"You live here now!" said Rodney. It was more of an order than a statement.

The peachick tried to hide behind a toy truck. Rodney kicked the truck aside.

"No hiding," said Betty. "You belong to us."

Plum gulped. Usually animals can be reasoned with. Once he had successfully convinced a pack of raccoons to leave the zoo. But the Bickles' dog did not seem reasonable. And the Bickle children . . . well, everyone knew what they were like.

Plum turned to the cats. "We need a plan."

"We might even need more help," said Jeremy.

Chapter Eight
The Sewers

Itch crept along a narrow ledge that ran beside the stream of sewage. The sewer system was smelly, dark, and very gloomy.

Itch paused.

Drip. Drip.

"Come out where I can see you," he called.

Something shifted ahead and then—

"Itch?"

A raccoon stepped out of the shadows.

"Clive!" said Itch.

"Gosh, you scared me," said Clive.

"What are you doing down here?" asked Itch.

"Visiting some friends," said Clive, who lived in the nearby Athensville Woods. "What are *you* doing here? Why aren't you at the zoo?"

"Plum needs to be rescued."

"Oh, no!" said Clive. "What happened?"

Itch filled Clive in. Clive considered.

"Well, I don't know where those kids live," Clive said. "But you are right; someone down here probably does."

"Is there an underworld ringleader? A big boss?" asked Itch.

"That's the thing," said Clive. "The sewer

is home to a lot of critters, and they're a bit disorganized."

Clive snapped his little fingers.

"I've got it!" said Clive. "I know who we can ask."

"Excellent," said Itch.

"But first . . . are you freaked-out by teeth?" asked Clive.

"How many teeth?" said Itch.

"A lot of teeth," said Clive.

This was not a time for fear. Itch followed Clive through a series of twisting, dark tunnels, deeper and deeper into the sewers. They climbed down a ladder into a large chamber flickering with the dim yellow light of a few electric bulbs.

Immediately Itch felt that they were being watched. And then he saw beady little eyes. Eyes everywhere. It was like a beady eye convention.

Itch took a step back. That's when he noticed something directly above him.

"Hello," said Itch to the small creature hanging from its tail.

"MA!" yelled the small creature.

"What?" another voice answered.

"Not you, Da! I need Ma!"

"What, Colin?" hollered a female voice. "You'll raise the play-dead with that racket."

A creature ambled out from behind some large pipes.

"Hey!" said Clive with a wave.

"Hello, Clive! It's been an age. Where've you been keeping yourself?"

"The woods, mostly," said Clive.

"Must be nice. And who will this be?"

"Itch," said Itch. "Ningbing of the Athensville Zoo."

"Oooh, fancy. I'll be Bridget Opossum of the Athensville Sewers," said the opossum.

"Nice to meet you," said Itch. "And . . ."

"My children," said Bridget, indicating the beady eyes blinking in the dark. "Colin, Liam, Polly, Tommy, Barry, Rosie, and Mary Pat."

"Hellooooo!" said the small ones as they came closer.

"Don't forget Da, Ma!" said Colin.

"Oh, right. Also my mate, Dan Opossum."

A portly opossum stuck his snout out from another pipe.

"All right?" asked Dan in a cheery manner.

"No, not all right," said Itch. "I need information."

"All business, aren't you?" said Bridget Opossum. "Is he always all business, Clive?"

"Yes, Itch is pretty focused," said Clive.

"I seem to recall hearing some tales about you," said Bridget. "From some raccoons and squirrels."

"I have, uh, worked with squirrels in the past," said Itch.

One of the little opossums dropped into the sewer water.

"Oh, for crying out loud, Barry!" shouted Bridget. "Polly, Tommy, get your brother out of the water. It's not bath night!"

Itch considered the idea of bathing in sewage water. It explained a few things about the appearance—and smell—of the creatures. Then he regained focus.

"I need to know the location of a human family,

the Bickles. Rodney and Betty are the so-called children."

Dan Opossum backed slowly behind the pipes. "Bad news, those kids."

"I know," said Itch. "But this is very important."

Bridget Opossum took a step closer to Itch. She stared into his eyes. Itch did not blink.

"No fear," said Bridget. "You must be quite a little feller to take on the Bickle brats."

Itch leaned in.

"I am a ningbing of many talents."

Bridget Opossum chuckled.

"You know what? I believe you. Come on, fam! Into the darkness!"

Chapter Nine
Cat Style

Plum paced beside the chain-link fence. It was too high to jump over, and it had spiky little metal things at the top.

"I don't think any of us can get over this fence," said Plum.

"I know a way in," said Bongo. "It's how I got out before."

"How?" asked Plum.

"See that pine tree behind the shed?"

Plum and Jeremy looked. The tree was a few feet outside the fence and taller than the shed.

"It's possible to jump from that tree over the fence and onto the shed. Then you can jump down into the yard," said Bongo.

"Really?" asked Plum.

"Well, a cat can," said Bongo.

"*Two* cats can," said Jeremy. "You're not going in there alone."

"It might get kind of dicey," said Bongo.

"That's why I'm going. I'm not letting my new friend face that dog alone."

Bongo blinked. "New friend?"

"Of course," said Jeremy. "We cool cats have to stick together."

"Yeah!" said Bongo. "Jeremy and Bongo! Bongo and Jeremy! Cats with names!"

"And Plum," added Plum.

"You can't make that jump, Plum," said Jeremy. "We need you out here for supervision. You know, keeping an eye on the situation."

"I know what it means," said Plum. "But I don't like this plan. Pip is my responsibility."

"We'll be in and out," said Bongo.

Plum stared at the yard. The Bickle brats had placed Pip in a plastic bucket. They had a handmade sign taped to a stick that read: BICKLES' ZOO: 10 DOLLARS 2 GET IN. They were hammering the stick into the dirt next to the bucket. Plum could hear Pip's worried chirps.

"Okay," said Plum. "Thank you."

Bongo and Jeremy climbed the pine tree and

inched along a branch. Plum checked the yard. The kids were busy with their sign. Brick appeared to be napping in a sunny spot. Plum gave them the all-clear signal.

The two cats leaped from the branch over the fence and onto the shed. Jeremy stumbled and clawed frantically as he slid down the roof. Bongo grabbed him before he fell.

Once they had regained their balance, they observed the scene.

"Lots of caution, then swift action," said Plum to himself.

The cats continued to stare.

"That's enough caution," said Plum.

Bongo yawned.

"Swift action time. Let's go," said Plum.

Jeremy whispered something to Bongo, who

nodded. Bongo slipped down the side of the shed.

He slinked along the fence. No one noticed. Bongo darted behind the piñata tree, just behind the Bickle brats.

Jeremy crept silently from the shed and coiled in position, ready to spring.

"Cats are really good at this kind of thing," said Plum with approval.

Bongo let out a soft meow. He was careful not to wake Brick, but it was loud enough to get the attention of Rodney and Betty. They looked over. Pip peeked out from the bucket.

Pip squeaked at the sight of Bongo and huddled at the bottom of the bucket.

"Pip!" called Plum. "It's okay! They're friends!"

Plum had chirped at top volume. The sound of a

peacock is unusual for a typical suburban backyard. Unusual enough to wake a German shepherd.

"BOWOWOWOWOWOW!" barked Brick.

"Come over here, little Pip!" said Jeremy from the shed. "I won't hurt you."

But Pip remained huddled in the bucket.

Brick jumped for Bongo, but the cat dodged the enormous dog.

"Jeremy!" called Bongo, slipping past Rodney as the boy grabbed for him.

Brick realized there were *two* cats. In *his* yard.

Brick charged Bongo. Bongo sprang straight up and grabbed hold of the unicorn piñata. Brick strained to reach him.

Jeremy snuck behind the dog and gave him a swipe with his claws. Brick yowled and turned to face him. Jeremy hopped on Brick's back and then up to the unicorn.

"Oh, no!" said
Plum.

The cats hung desperately
to the piñata, spinning slowly
above the snapping jaws of the
dog.

And that's when Rodney hit the
piñata with a stick.

The unicorn piñata tumbled down.

Fortunately it landed on Brick. Bongo and
Jeremy sprinted to the bucket.

Pip wasn't there. She had tipped the bucket
and was now hiding in the shed from the dog, the
cats, and the brats.

"Come out, little chick!" begged Bongo.

Pip disappeared behind some boxes.

"Retreat!" called Plum from his hiding place in the bushes.

The cats climbed an old bike and scrambled to the roof just before Brick slammed into the bike, knocking it to the ground.

Jeremy and Bongo jumped from the roof to the pine tree, barely clearing the fence.

Brick continued to bark. Plum sat down in a frustrated heap.

"Now what?" said Plum.

The Bickle brats searched for Pip in the shed but could not find her. Their mother came out and called the kids for dinner. They closed the shed door and went into the house.

Brick circled a spot three times, lay down, and fell fast asleep.

Plum stood. He knew what he had to do.

**Chapter Ten
A New Opportunity**

Itch hurried down what seemed like the hundredth dank passage.

"How big is this sewer system?" Itch asked Clive, who was beside him.

"Very," said Clive. "It runs under all of Athensville. Even I get lost down here."

"Are we almost at the Bickle residence?" Itch

asked Bridget Opossum, who was leading the way.

"Yes, of course," said Bridget. She stopped, and all of her children and Dan Opossum banged into her.

Itch and Clive slowed to a stop. Itch noticed that the rescue party had grown with each passage they had taken. Rats, raccoons, snakes, and mice were all trooping behind them.

Bridget addressed the crowd. "Are we all here, then?"

The sewer critters answered yes.

"Right," said Bridget. "The gang is all here, Itch."

At the mention of Itch's name, many of the critters began to murmur to one another.

"You're sort of famous, Itch," said Dan Opossum.

"I am?" asked Itch. "How?"

"Well," said Clive, "I think some of the raccoons have been telling the stories they heard about you at Shindigs. The squirrels, too."

"I'm flattered," said Itch. "But we must continue."

"Whatever you say," said Bridget. She smiled, showing her many, many teeth.

No one moved.

Itch glanced around. They seemed to be waiting for something.

"Um . . . ONWARD!" Itch yelled.

The possums, rats, raccoons, snakes, and mice all marched through yet another tunnel. On they went. Eventually they stopped below a ladder.

"Here we are," said Bridget.

Itch scampered up the ladder, through a short passage, and then finally up through a sewer opening on the surface.

A busy supermarket stood in front of him. No houses. Just a parking lot and a supermarket.

"What's this?" said Itch.

"Opportunity!" said Bridget, sticking her snout out from the sewer opening.

"I asked you to take me to the Bickle house," said Itch. "Not shopping."

Itch hopped back down into the sewer, and Bridget followed. They joined the others.

"Clive, what is this?" demanded Itch.

"No idea," said the raccoon. "Bridget, Itch needs—"

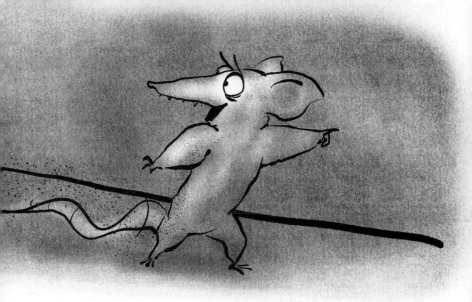

"*We* need *Itch*," said Bridget.

"What are you talking about?" said Itch. He was beginning to notice exactly how many critters had gathered in the sewer.

"That supermarket is a gold mine," said Bridget. "Rows of food for the taking! We need someone clever to devise the perfect heist!"

"A heist?" said Itch.

"Or a series of heists," said Dan Opossum. "Whatever you think is best. We need a leader,

Itch. We're a bit disorganized, to say the least."

"I must find Plum and return him to the zoo. That is my charge, my responsibility," said Itch.

"But what about after that?" asked Bridget.

Itch paused. The underworld creatures seemed so eager to learn from him. It was clear that they would *hang on his every word, ready to follow his lead without question.*

"We shall see," said Itch. "Now take me to the Bickle house."

"He's so decisive," squeaked little Mary Pat Opossum.

"A born mastermind," said a scraggly rat.

"This way, O leader of the underworld," said Bridget with a wink.

Chapter Eleven
The Only Way

Plum's plan came to him quickly. Pip only trusted Plum. So Plum had to be the rescuer. And now that the cats had failed, everyone agreed to let him try.

"Okay," said Plum. "This is how we do it."

Ever since Pip had been taken from the zoo, Plum's brain had been buzzing with noise, as if several radio stations were playing at once. And over the noise his brain was yelling, "Get Pip! Get Pip!"

But now the noise was gone. His brain was quiet. He could see solutions that had been hidden moments before. He was excited, but also calm.

Plum was focused.

"Do you see that sickly tree on the other side of the yard?" asked Plum.

"Outside the fence?" asked Jeremy.

"Yes, we're going to climb it."

The cats followed Plum without another word. Plum hopped up to a low branch, then up a few more, just like he was climbing the Great Tree back at the zoo. The cats climbed behind him.

"Here is how I'll get in," said Plum. "And how Pip and I will get back out."

Plum inched out onto a very thin branch. It dipped slightly under his weight.

"Now," said Plum. "You two climb carefully onto this branch, too. The extra weight will lower me into the yard. Then you go back and the branch will rise again."

"And we lower it again after you get Pip!" said Jeremy.

"Right," said Plum. "Easy peasy."

"Brick is still asleep," said Bongo. "We should go now."

"Ready when you are," said Plum.

The cats nodded. They carefully walked out onto the limb, lowering Plum into the yard. He hopped down.

Plum kept an eye on the sleeping dog. He took a step.

The dog stirred.

Plum froze.

Brick settled down.

Plum took a step.

The dog snorted.

Plum hit the ground and rolled behind the unicorn piñata.

Brick looked up, eyes half open. He snorted again, then fell back asleep.

Plum had wriggled inside the empty piñata. He slowly got to his feet again. And wobbled across the yard as quietly as possible.

He reached the shed and wriggled out of the piñata.

"Pip!" Plum whispered through the door. "It's me, Plum. I'm here to rescue you."

For a moment there was silence. And then Plum heard a tiny scratching sound and a hopeful: "Pip?"

"That's right," said Plum. "We're going to toodle pip out of here and go home to the zoo."

"Pip! Pip!"

"You have to be quiet," said Plum. "We don't want to wake the nice doggo."

Rrrrrrrrr.

Plum slowly looked behind him.

Brick was wide awake, crouched and growling low.

"Oooookay," said Plum. "Listen, I—"

Brick charged. Plum leaped out of the way a split second before Brick crashed into the shed door, knocking it open.

Plum raced around the shed. Brick ran after him. Plum flapped his wings and sailed over the fallen bicycle, but Brick wasn't as quick-thinking. The dog collided with the bike.

Plum raced back to the open shed door.

"Hop on!" he yelled.

Pip hopped onto Plum's back, and they ran for the tree.

The cats lowered the branch, and Plum and Pip jumped on. The cats backed up, and the branch began to rise.

Suddenly Brick jumped up and bit the end of the branch. He shook the branch so hard that it snapped, sending Plum and Pip crashing to the ground. Instantly Plum was back up with Pip clinging to his back. They ran with Brick in hot pursuit.

Plum headed for the long, yellow plastic strip that lay at the center of the yard. It was wet, it was slippery, and Plum and Pip slid down it at top speed.

"Yikes!" yelled Plum. "Hold on!"

"Pip! Pip!"

Brick also ran onto the yellow strip and once again proved that dogs are not the most graceful of creatures. His legs slipped out from under him. He flopped forward and slid on his belly.

The strip ended at the back porch. Plum watched as he got closer and closer and—

Hop! Off he went with Pip holding tight.

Brick collided into the deck with a tremendous CRASH.

"What's going on?"

Rodney and Betty ran out the back door.

"Is he after a raccoon?" asked an excited Betty.

The Bickle brats stared at Plum.

"Wow!" said Rodney.

"A full-grown peacock!" said Betty.

"In *our* backyard!" said Rodney.

"A chick *and* a grown-up!" said Betty. "Bickles' Zoo is going to be famous!"

Brick growled.

"STAY," yelled Rodney and Betty.

Brick sat down and lowered his head. Rodney took a leash that was attached to the porch and clicked it onto Brick's collar.

Plum backed away from the children. Jeremy and Bongo watched from the high branches of the tree.

"Just look at that thing," said Rodney.

"Sooo cool," said Betty. "I bet we can charge *twenty* dollars for our zoo now!"

Plum's mind raced. Pip held on to his feathers. Plum backed up and stepped on something plastic. It was attached to a tube that connected to a toy rocket.

Once more, Plum's mind focused.

He kept his eye on the kids.

"Check out the feathers," said Rodney.

"You haven't seen anything yet," said Plum.

WHOOSH!

Out came Plum's full plumage, a rather impressive display of tail feathers.

"WHOA!" said both kids, stopping in their tracks.

"Pip, hop down," whispered Plum.

Pip dropped onto Plum's wing as Plum turned on the spot. His tail feathers now blocked the kids' view.

Plum placed Pip on the toy rocket.

"Grip this tight," said Plum. "Hold on and don't be scared."

"Pip!" Pip did as she was told.

Plum turned again to face the kids, his tail still hiding Pip and the rocket. Plum stood on top of the plastic rocket launcher. But he wasn't heavy enough to launch it.

"Come and get me," said Plum.

The Bickle brats sprang and tackled Plum. The

weight of all three pressing down on the launcher

sent a blast of air through the tube, and the rocket

and Pip shot high into the air.

Then the rocket arced gracefully toward the

tree. Jeremy raced down a branch, reached out—

and caught the rocket and Pip!

"Great catch!" yelled Bongo.

The kids held Plum on the ground, but looked up when they heard the yowling cat.

"Hey!" said Betty.

"Aw, who cares if the cat eats the chick," said Rodney. "The big one has the cool tail."

"Yeah! We need the big one for our zoo," agreed Betty.

Plum looked up at Jeremy and Bongo from under the Bickle brats.

"Go, Jeremy!" called Plum. "Take Pip home!"

"But, Plum," said Jeremy.

"I'll be okay," said Plum. "They won't try to get you if they have me. It's the only way."

And Plum knew this was true. So did the cats.

"Come on," said Bongo quietly. "He's right."

Jeremy stared down at his friend. Then he gently placed Pip onto his back.

Pip started chirping and pointing at Plum.

"It will be fine," said Plum. "You can go."

"Pip!"

"Yes," said Plum. "Toodle pip . . . to everybody."

The Bickle brats picked Plum up, took him into the shed, and shut the door. They unleashed Brick to stand guard.

The cats climbed down from the tree with the peachick. Jeremy took one last look at the shed before starting the journey back to the zoo.

Plum climbed a crate and watched through the dirty window as his friends escaped.

Then he sat down and stared at the walls of the shed.

His new home.

Chapter Twelve
A Sad Tale to Tell

Itch and Clive had followed the underworld critters through a labyrinth of sewer passages. They had to stop and retrace steps often. It had taken a very long time.

"Bridget," huffed Itch. "Are we almost—"

"There!" shouted Bridget, screeching to a halt. All of her tired little ones clung to her back.

"Through that opening," said Bridget. "You will find . . ."

Itch climbed to the surface.

"The Athensville Zoo," he said quietly.

For that is exactly where they were. It was dark now, and the zoo was long closed. They had brought Itch back to where he began.

"Oh, sweet muffins," said Bridget, climbing out with the others. "I am sorry, Itch."

"I told you we were disorganized," said Dan Opossum.

"Itch," said Clive. "We'll try something else. I'll talk to Scratch and the other raccoons. I bet someone knows how to get to the Bickle house."

"I fear it might be too late," said Itch.

He was staring across the street. Jeremy and Bongo slowly approached the walls of the zoo. Pip was riding on Jeremy's back.

When they reached Itch, Jeremy told the group everything—all about the yard, the vicious dog, the rescue attempts, Plum's sacrifice, and how he had insisted they take Pip home. Plum was not returning.

Itch nodded. "Let's get the little one to her parents. I'll take her through the chipmunk entrance. Clive, thank you for your help."

Clive sniffed.

"Itch," said Bridget Opossum. "I am truly sorry about Plum, but what about us? Come and lead us!"

"I am honored, Bridget," said Itch. "You have a fine underworld crew. And although you are *desperately* in need of leadership, I am not the ningbing for the job."

"You are!" said Dan. "We just know it!"

"My place is here at the zoo," said Itch. "Especially now. There will be a great deal of sadness, and I must help where I can. My responsibility is to my friends."

"I think they're more than your friends, Itch," said Bridget Opossum. "This zoo is your family."

Itch looked over at the two cats and the tired little peachick.

"You're right," said Itch. "My family."

"Nothing is more important than that," said Bridget, making sure her little ones were all holding tight.

The opossums, rats, snakes, and mice returned to the sewer opening.

"If you change your mind, you know where to find us," called Bridget, disappearing down the sewer. "More or less."

"Itch," said Jeremy, letting Pip off his back, "tell Meg. Right away."

"Of course," said Itch.

Jeremy and Bongo said good night, and Jeremy invited Bongo to Lizzie's apartment. Clive set off for the woods. Itch led Pip through the small passage in the wall and returned her to her worried parents at the Great Tree.

And then he told Meg what had happened to Plum.

Chapter Thirteen
Second Chances

Plum sat in the cool, dark shed. Ever since the Bickle kids were called in for the night, Plum had been thinking about his situation.

"Maybe I could convince them to paint the inside a nice color," said Plum, looking at the shed walls. "Or . . . *a* color."

He sighed. Plum normally had no trouble

seeing the positive in any situation. He was a peppy, glass-half-full kind of peacock. But there was no getting around this. He was trapped, hidden away by two not-nice children.

Plum stared at the sky through his window. No stars out tonight.

There was a scratch at the door, and it creaked open.

Brick the dog stood in the doorway.

Plum gulped.

Brick snorted and stared at Plum for a few tense seconds.

"Follow me," he said.

Confused, Plum followed the dog outside and around the shed. In the back some bushes stood right against the fence.

Brick pointed his nose at a small opening in a bush. Plum peered through. A large hole had been dug under the fence.

"Go on," said Brick.

Plum glanced from the hole to the dog.

"Are you coming, too?" asked Plum.

"No," said Brick.

Brick scratched at the dirt for a moment. He looked back at the house. Through a lit window on the second floor, they could see Rodney and Betty, bouncing on a bed.

"I remember when they were younger," said Brick softly. "They were sweet. Both of them. They can be a little bratty these days, but . . ."

He turned back to Plum.

"I believe those sweet kids are still in there somewhere. Maybe their old dog can help bring them back."

"I bet you can," said Plum.

Brick nodded and snorted again.

"Thank you, Brick," said Plum as he climbed through the hole and under the fence.

"Good luck," said Brick, and he trotted back to the house.

Plum eyed the dark street.

"Good luck," he muttered to himself.

Plum walked. He walked and walked. He had no idea where the zoo was. He couldn't even find the dump. The hours crawled, and Plum was so tired he was nearly crawling, too. He stopped to rest on the steps of the Athensville Library.

"Well, Plum," he said to himself. "You're free . . . but lost."

Plum could see a nearby park. He didn't think

it was the woods, where he had friends, but it was a big park with lots of trees. Maybe he could find a place to live there.

A place to live. Not a *home*.

Plum had never felt so alone. In fact, he had never really been alone before at all. There were always zookeepers like Lizzie, zoo visitors, and the other animals: Kevin, Mike the alligator, Itch, and—most importantly—the peacock flock.

There was always—*always*—Meg, his best friend since they were peachicks.

He sniffled and began to climb a hill. When he reached the top, he could see the center of town, the houses, the parks, the local schools . . . and the Athensville Zoo.

His heart soared. The zoo! The *zoo*!

Plum raced down the hill toward the zoo,

skipping over curbs and turning down side streets, feeling more energy than he had all night.

And then he was outside the great walls of his home.

The walls towered over the small peacock who stood in their shadow. The walls with locked gates. The walls that kept him out of his home. They had never seemed so high before.

It was silent outside the dark zoo. A chilly wind blew. Plum touched the wall with his wing. There was no way he could climb it. There was no way to get in.

Plum turned from the wall and began to walk away, back to the shelter of the nearby park. Maybe he could—

"PLUM!"

Plum stopped and looked back.

Itch was jumping up and down by a small crack in the wall. He ran toward Plum.

"Itch!" called Plum. He couldn't believe his eyes.

Itch abruptly stopped, then raced back to the wall, disappearing once more through the crack.

"Itch?" asked Plum. Had he really seen him? Was he dreaming?

Itch raced through the passage back into the zoo. Meg was there. He told her what he'd seen, and she bolted across the zoo. She stopped below the Great Tree and bellowed: "It's Plum! He needs our help."

Instantly peacocks dropped from the branches of the Great Tree. Big and small, young and old, they all followed Meg back.

Kevin raced along the habitrail, skidding to a stop near the wall. He could see Plum.

"They're coming!" Kevin yelled.

"Who?" asked Plum.

"Everyone!"

The peacocks gathered at the base of the wall. The biggest one bent down and another climbed on his back. Then another climbed up and another and another.

Finally Meg hopped up to the top of the wall and waved.

"Hiya, Fun Plum!"

"Meg!"

"We'll get you in a jiffy," said Meg.

More peacocks scrambled up the wall. Then they leaned over, making a long chain of outstretched wings and talons. They lowered down, down . . .

"Easy now," directed Itch. "That's right. Just like I explained it to you. Steady!"

Plum stretched up and caught hold of the outstretched talon belonging to Bill the peacock. He climbed up on the backs of his friends to reach the top. Each peacock did the same until they were all on top of the wall again. Then they reversed the process until they were on firm ground inside the zoo. The flock collapsed in an exhausted heap of feathers.

Plum was, for the first time ever, speechless.

"Welcome home," said Meg.

Chapter Fourteen
A Bright New Day

The next morning was gloriously sunny and warm, with the smell of blooming flowers and lilac bushes throughout the Athensville Zoo.

Plum and Meg strolled the grounds before the Mandatory Morning Meeting. On the way they ran into Lizzie, who told them how Jeremy had escaped during the day (bad!) but had returned later that night, to her great relief. *And* he had brought a stray cat with him. The two seemed to get along well, so Lizzie had decided to keep the new cat.

"I think I'll call him Bongo," said Lizzie. "It just seems to fit somehow."

Plum and Meg joined the flock at the meeting. All of the chicks played in the front, peeping and pipping happily.

"Last night was quite extraordinary," said Hampstead. "And I am proud of each and every one of you."

"Pip!"

"Yes, you are quite right, little one," said Hampstead. "There is indeed one peacock who deserves special mention." Hampstead paused. "Is Plum here, by the way?"

"Of course I'm here!" said Plum. "Everyone

knows this meeting is mandatory!"

"Hmmph," said Hampstead. "I will continue then. As head peacock, I formally recognize Plum for extraordinary bravery, exemplary responsibility, and selfless dedication to the flock."

"Hear! Hear!" shouted the peacocks.

Hampstead walked over to Plum and said quietly, "I am so glad you are back."

"Me, too," said Plum.

"In celebration," said Hampstead, raising his voice again, "I am canceling today's Mandatory Morning Meeting!"

"GASP!" gasped the peacocks.

"And in its stead, I suggest a parade of peacocks through the entire grounds of the Athensville Zoo!" proclaimed Hampstead.

"HUZZAH!" shouted the peacocks.

"Plum, will you take the lead?" said Hampstead.

"Well," said Plum.

"What is it?" asked Meg.

"Maybe I'll march in the back," said Plum. "So I can keep an eye on every—"

Hampstead and Meg looked at him.

"Oh, who am I kidding?" said Plum, racing to the front of the parade. "Follow me!"

The peacocks marched through the zoo, greeting all the animals and zookeepers. They chirped happily and displayed their plumage and brought cheer to all they passed.

The doors to the Small and Unusual Mammal Pavilion were open, letting in the morning breeze. Plum led the parade inside to Itch's cage.

Itch sat meditating with his eyes closed.

"Peep! Peep! Peep! Peep! Pip!" said the chicks.

Itch opened one eye. "Yes?" he said.

"Good morning, Itch!" said Plum. "We're having a parade!"

"Swell," said Itch.

"Wish you could join us," said Meg.

"Alas," said Itch, closing his eyes again.

"But I know what you *can* do," said Plum.

Itch opened his eyes. "Do I have to?"

"Yep!"

"The things I do for this zoo," said Itch.

"All together now!" said Plum.

And Plum, Meg, Hampstead, the entire

peacock flock, *and* Itch shouted out the sacred

duties of the Athensville Zoo family:

"MINGLE! GUIDE! DELIGHT!"

And that is exactly what they did.